This Book Belongs to

Visit us on the Web! randomhousekids.com

Educators and librarians, for a variety of teaching tools, visit us at RHTeachersLibrarians.com

Library of Congress Cataloging-in-Publication Data
Martin, Emily Winfield, author, illustrator.
The wonderful things you will be / Emily Winfield Martin. — First edition.
pages cm.
Summary: Illustrations and simple, rhyming text reveal a parent's musings about what a child will become,
knowing that the child's kindness, cleverness, and boldness will shine through no matter what, as will the love they share.
ISBN 978-0-385-37671-6 (trade) — ISBN 978-0-375-97327-7 (lib. bdg.) — ISBN 978-0-375-98218-7 (ebook)
[1. Stories in rhyme. 2. Parent and child—Fiction.] I. Title.
PZ8.3.M418Won 2015 [E]—dc23 2014023314

MANUFACTURED IN CHINA
11
First Edition

For Nicole de las Heras,
who makes our books Wonderful

The Wonderful Things You Will Be

Emily Winfield Martin

Random House New York

When I look at you
And you look at me,
I wonder what wonderful
Things you will be.

When you were too small
To tell me hello,
I knew you were someone
I wanted to know.

For all of your tininess
Couldn't disguise
A heart so enormous . . .

And wild . . .

and wise.

This is the first time

There's ever been *you,*

So I wonder what wonderful things

You will do.

Will you stand up for good
By saving the day?

Or play a song only you
Know how to play?

Will you tell a story

That only you know?

Will you learn what it means
To help things to grow?

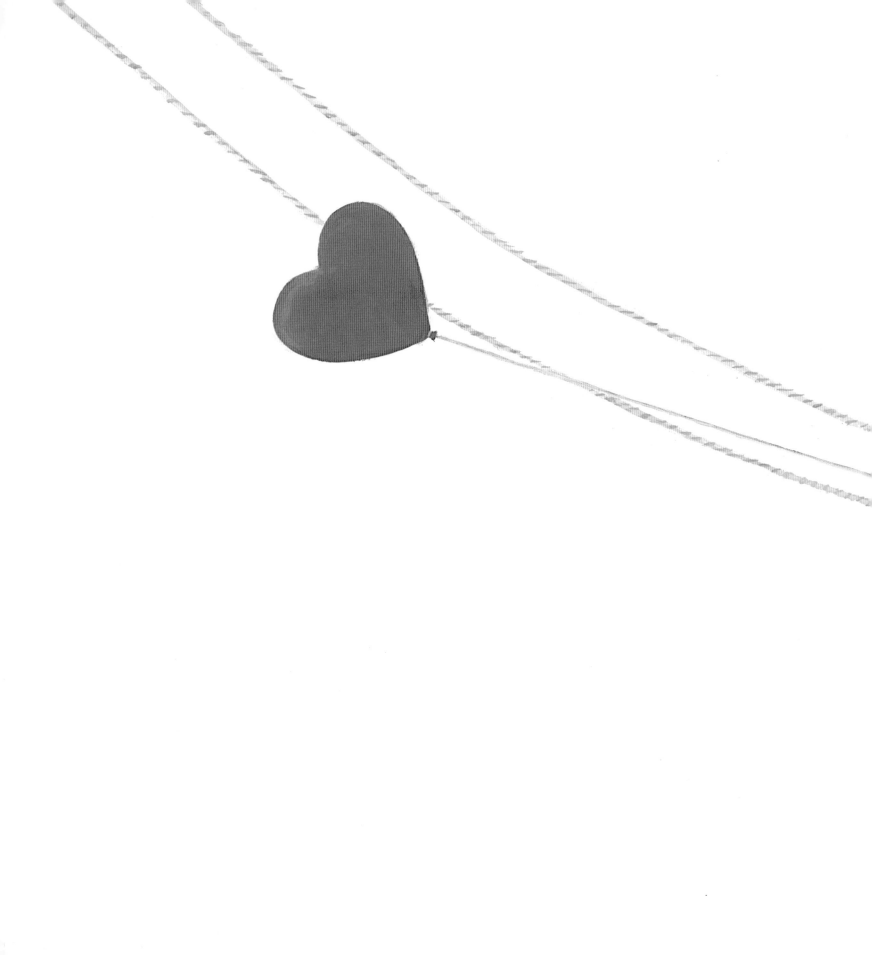

Will you learn how to fly
To find the best view?

Or take care of things

Much smaller than you?

I know you'll be kind . . .

And clever . . .

and bold.

And the bigger your heart,
The more it will hold.

When nights are black and
When days are gray—
You'll be brave and be bright
So no shadows can stay.

Then you will discover
All there is to see . . .

And become *anybody*
That you'd like to be.

And then I'll look at you
And you'll look at me
And I'll love you,
Whoever you've grown up to be.